William B. Swett

Adventures of a Deaf-Mute

William B. Swett

Adventures of a Deaf-Mute

ISBN/EAN: 9783337339500

Printed in Europe, USA, Canada, Australia, Japan

Cover: Foto ©Raphael Reischuk / pixelio.de

More available books at **www.hansebooks.com**

ADVENTURES

OF A

DEAF-MUTE.

THE OLD MAN OF THE MOUNTAIN.

PUBLISHED FOR THE

BOSTON DEAF-MUTES' MISSION,

LIBRARY ROOM, 289 WASHINGTON STREET.

1874.

DEAF - MUTE.

THE OLD MAN OF THE MOUNTAIN.

PUBLISHED FOR THE

BOSTON DEAF-MUTES' MISSION,

LIBRARY ROOM, 289 WASHINGTON STREET.

1871.

INTRODUCTION.

MANY persons who visited the White Mountains of New Hampshire, and particularly the Profile House, in 1866, and later years, will readily recognize the hero of these adventures, and the incidents connected therewith, and will doubtless bear testimony to their truth. The measuring of "The Old Stone Face," and the placing of the images of the "Panther" and the "Indian" upon Eagle Cliff, will be remembered as hazardous adventures successfully accomplished, and Mr. WILLIAM B. SWETT has the honor of their achievement.

Born at Henniker, N. H., in 1824, with the full use of all his senses, but losing his hearing while yet a lad, he was sent to the Institution for the Deaf and Dumb at Hartford, Conn., and after completing the usual course of studies there, returned to his home, and for awhile pursued the calling of his father,— that of a carpenter and joiner. His capacity as a ready and faithful workman procured him permanent work at the Mountains, where his restless and adventurous spirit brought him into many awkward and dangerous positions, from which, however, he always emerged right-side up.

A ready thinker, and fluent in the use of the sign language, his talents have brought him, of late, into other pursuits, having in view the welfare and improvement of his fellow-unfortunates. Prominent in all such movements, he became interested in several societies of Deaf-Mutes, among which are the BOSTON DEAF-MUTES' LIBRARY ASSOCIATION, and the BOSTON DEAF-MUTE MISSION. This volume is published and the profits will be devoted to the purposes of the "Mission," whose object is to provide for the religious welfare of Deaf-Mutes. With this "Mission" Mr. Swett is now more particularly identified, and issues this narrative of his Adventures in the hope that a large sum may inure to the benefit of this much-needed and now prosperous enterprise. All purchasers will therefore understand that they are aiding directly in the promotion of the highest interests of Deaf-Mutes.

H. W. S.

(iii)

WM. B. SWETT,
White Mountain Adventurer.

ADVENTURES

OF A

DEAF-MUTE IN THE WHITE MOUNTAINS.

FIRST SUMMER.

HOW I HAPPENED TO GO TO THE MOUNTAINS.

EARLY in the year 1865, the proprietors of the Profile House, in the Franconia Mountains, finding repairs and additions necessary to their hotel, advertised for a large gang of workmen.

I received a pressing invitation to go up and work. The wages were good, and expenses paid both ways.

I hesitated,—there was work enough at home; I had never been out of work a single day, having always been sought for to do all kinds of work both in and out of town. I was acknowledged to be a skilful and steady workman. I hesitated, also, because my family and myself had been thrown into deep mourning by the recent death, from diphtheria, of two of our children, our only boy and a girl; but after a few days of reflection and consultation with my family, I decided to go.

I may as well say here, that, while the wages offered were very acceptable, they had not so much to do with my decision as had a desire to see a place of which I had heard so much, and an idea that there would be some chance to gratify my love of adventure.

Of adventure I subsequently had a good deal, as will be shown in the course of my story.

I notified several persons, who were waiting for me to do some work for them, that they must find some one else to do it, as I must go. They told me that they would wait until my return; and, bidding my family good-by, I was whirled away over the iron track.

At Concord, N. H., while waiting for the train from Boston, I noticed a strange-looking old man in the depot. His hair and beard were long and white, giving him a very patriarchal look.

The day was very cold, but he wore a straw hat and thin summer clothes, and his neck and feet were bare. He walked about with great activity, taking snuff frequently from a bladder, which served him in-

(5)

stead of a box. He looked sharply at every one, and spoke to me once ; but when I put a finger to my ear and shook my head, he walked away. I wondered who and what he was, and inclined to think him either insane or very odd. I have since seen him going about the streets of Concord barefooted, and dressed in thin clothes, when the snow lay a foot deep on the ground.

His name is Flagg ; he lives in a log cabin at Pembroke, about fifteen miles from Concord. He professes to be a water-cure doctor, and is about seventy-five years old.

Speculation in the various forms in which human nature crops out, helped me to pass away the time till the train came along.

Before reaching Lake Village, the train stopped at a small station for a supply of wood and water. Here a very ragged and dirty little boy annoyed the passengers by passing up and down in the cars. Meeting the conductor, a large and powerful man, he pushed past him and would have gone out, but the conductor seized him and actually threw him out of a window upon a wood-car that was slowly moving in an opposite direction. This little incident made every one roar with laughter. The boy was not hurt, though he was probably somewhat frightened.

After passing Lake Village, I caught my first glimpse of the peak of Mount Washington, the highest of all the White Mountains. Its summit was wrapped in snow, and its sublime appearance gave me much food for thought.

As we rode along, I caught occasional glimpses of sheets of water, and at last the broad and beautiful Lake Winnipiseogee lay before me. I no longer wondered at the name given it by the Indians, if, as some say, it means "The Smile of the Great Spirit." It has been called the "Loch Lomond" of America.

Loch Lomond is a lake in Scotland, famous for its beauty, but it is generally admitted, by those who have seen both, that Winnipiseogee is the most beautiful of the two.

The late Hon. Edward Everett, speaking of a visit to this lake, said : "I have been something of a traveller in our own country, though not so much as I could wish, and in Europe have seen all that is most attractive, from the Highlands of Scotland to the Golden Horn of Constantinople, from the summit of the Hartz Mountains to the Fountain of Vaucluse ; but my eye has yet to rest on a lovelier scene than that which smiles around you as you sail from Weir's Landing to Centre Harbor."

At the Pemigewasset House, in Plymouth, where the train stopped for dinner, I met that prince of good fellows, Hiram Bell, Esq., the landlord of the hotel ; formerly the well-known and popular landlord of the Profile House. It was to him that I was indebted for the invitation to go and work in the Mountains.

The deaf-mutes who composed the party which visited the Profile House and went up Mount Lafayette, in 1858, will remember Mr. Bell as a liberal-hearted man and a genial friend. I shall elsewhere give an account of the adventures of this party, in connection with my own.

As the train neared Well's River, I was standing at the car door, looking out, and saw one of the car wheels fly off and roll down the bank. The next instant there was a terrible jarring; the stove-pipe was shaken out, and the passengers were thrown into confusion. I could hardly keep my feet, and concluded that I should be killed.

Some one gave the signal to "brake up" by pulling the cord that ran through the train, and it was stopped without accident. After this we moved slowly to the next stopping-place, where the damaged car was removed and the train sped on.

In due time I reached Littleton, from which place are stages to all parts of the Mountains. I was so anxious to secure a seat on the top of the stage, that I climbed upon it first and gave orders about my baggage afterwards.

Our six stout horses carried us along at a good rate; on the way, I had a fine view of the Mountains. One of the passengers pointed out Mount Lafayette to me. The day was clear, and I could see that snow was falling on the mountain-top, while below it was the vast, black ravine in which I afterwards nearly lost my life, of which I tell in the proper place.

After passing Franconia, noted for its iron mine, and as being one of the coldest places in the country, we saw a snow-storm coming down upon us, and for a few moments it completely enveloped and blinded us; when it cleared away, Mount Lafayette looked more majestic than before, in its mantle of white.

All symptoms of life, except ourselves, soon disappeared, and for some miles the road was through a gloomy forest, and at the end of this we arrived at the Profile House.

Few of us having been prepared for the storm and cold, the fire and a hot supper were very welcome indeed.

My signs and gestures, and my little slate, of which I made free use in talking with my companions, soon attracted the attention of the company, to most of whom a deaf-mute was evidently a new thing. One man in particular, an Irishman, who was seated in a corner smoking a pipe, after eyeing me intently for some time, approached me, laid a hand on my shoulder, looked me in the face, and then, making the sign of the cross, he nodded, went back to his seat, and resumed his pipe, apparently satisfied that it was all right. I could not help smiling at his behavior, and did not know what to think of it; but have since concluded that it was his way of either getting acquainted or of expressing sympathy.

I retired to bed, but could not sleep; my new situation and my own thoughts kept me awake. I could feel the house shake from the action of the wind, which was blowing hard, and, gathering extraordinary strength from compression in its passage through the Notch, struck with great force upon the hotel, which, although a very large building, shook like a person with the ague.

In the morning I was quite sick, having caught a bad cold in my ride from Littleton. After breakfast I felt better, and took a walk; the mountains, trees, rocks, and everything were covered with ice—the effect of the frost-clouds during the night—and in the rays of the rising sun everything glittered and glowed with all the colors of the rainbow. It was a magnificent sight; I thought of the fairy scenes in the " Arabian Nights."

The scene increased in beauty as the sun rose higher, till the frost-work began to dissolve in the warmth, and in a short time everything had returned to its usual dark and sombre hue.

My next thought was to visit the "Great Stone Face." "The Old Man of the Mountain."

" The Old Man of the Mountain."

I had heard much of this great natural curiosity, and had thought that there must be some resemblance to a human profile, but I was not prepared for the " accurate chiselling and astonishing sculpture " which now met my eyes.

The " Profile " has " a stern, projecting, massive brow, which looks as if it contained the thought and wisdom of centuries." The nose is " straight, and finely cut." The lips are thin, and slightly parted, as if about to speak. The chin is " well thrown forward, and shows the hard, obstinate character of the ' Old Man,' who has faced the storms of ages with such unmoving steadiness."

As I stood there, and looked at the towering cliff on which the " Old Man " is situated, all my appreciation of the grand and sublime in nature was awakened; and, mingled with other thoughts, came longings for a closer acquaintance with the " Old Man," and dreams of " doing and daring " in those wild regions as none had ever done before.

To the general observer, who sees the " Old Man " against a clear sky, the expression is one of earnest expectation, mingled with that " heart-sickness produced by hope long deferred." But the expression varies with the weather. Sometimes it appears on the point of giving utterance to speech ; sometimes it wears a settled scowl, and at others a look of more than mortal sadness.

Clouds passing under the chin or above and around the forehead materially soften the expression, and, by bearding and wigging the face, make it very lifelike. The best time to see it is in the afternoon, when the sun is behind it. After a cold rain, I have seen the " Old Man's " face glisten beautifully, and wear a smiling look.

During the four seasons which I have spent at the " Profile House," I have studied the " Old Man " in all its aspects as seen from below. It had a fascination for me which drew me to it in storm and in calm, by day and by night, in season and out of season. It was a strange and unaccountable influence and an irresistible impulse.

Often as I have looked upon the " Old Man," both far and near, I am not satisfied ; it still has the old attraction for me, and I hope to continue my researches in the vicinity.

Returning to the hotel, I spent the rest of the day in looking out of the windows upon the grand scenery with which it is surrounded, and in recalling to mind the mountain adventures and narrow escapes of which I had read, and trying to remember how the persons concerned acted, in order to escape the danger they were in.

I always had a love of adventure, but made it a rule " never to get into danger until I had planned how to get out of it " ; and I think it very important and useful for people to study and remember *how to act* in case of exposure to any kind of danger. If this were more generally practised, there would be much less loss of life. A person with presence of mind has an immense advantage in case of accidents, and is worth a hundred who are wild and distracted. Knowledge how to act has saved my own life and limbs several times.

The next day I was able to go to work, and was much amused by the whisperings and pointings of my fellow-workmen. They regarded me, for some time, as a strange person, and seemed to be much afraid of my slate and pencil. One of them, who stood near me one day when I pulled out my slate for some purpose, ran away as fast as possible, showing fear on his face ; but whether in fun or earnest I did not know, nor did I care, so long as there was nothing offensive in the manner. In course of time they got over this, and treated me as one of themselves.

The Bowling Alley at the foot of Cannon Mountain, so called, had been entirely destroyed, and we were ordered to rebuild it.

It was destroyed in the following manner :

It snowed for half a day, then a cold rain followed, which froze solid ; then fell a foot of snow, and the next day was so warm that the snow melted, and not being absorbed by the frozen ground, ran down the mountain into the valley. Gulches and ravines were quickly flooded : brooks became rivers, and cascades grew to cataracts. Behind the alley ran a small brook, which, overflowing its banks, undermined it and swept it away. The hotel grounds were flooded, all the cellars filled with water, and much damage was done. After finishing the alley, we were put to shingling the Profile House, the size of which may be imagined from its taking eight men twelve days to finish the front side only, and on that alone they used fifty thousand feet of shingles.

Snow-balling in June.

One warm day in June, I made one of a party of eight persons which ascended Cannon Mountain in search of quartz crystals, the distance being about a mile and a half.

It was my first experience in climbing mountains, and I was soon very tired. The path had been damaged by the spring freshets, and the ascent, hard at any time, was then unusually so.

The day was fine, but just as we reached the top of the mountain we were enveloped in clouds, and could neither go for the crystals or enjoy the fine view which can be had in clear weather.

We were obliged cautiously to retrace our steps, lest we should lose our way. I was much disappointed, but comforted myself by the reflection that I could come again.

As we were descending, we saw, a short distance to one side of the path, a patch of snow, about an acre in extent and a foot deep, so situated in a hollow that the sun never shone upon it. We left the path and went toward it: while looking around, some one proposed a little fun. With the feelings of younger days, the members of the party, whose ages ranged from thirty-five to sixty, divided into equal bodies and took up positions, the agreement being to pelt each other until one party should be driven from the snow.

The snow was soft, and easily worked, and the snow-balls flew fast and furious for more than an hour, when the party to which I belonged were driven from the field by a skilful movement of the other party, under the lead of an old gentleman of sixty, whose tactics would have been useful on a more earnest battle-field, and obliged to surrender.

The severe exercise had stirred our blood and put us in good humor, doing much to compensate us for the loss of our original object in coming up the Mountain; and we resumed our homeward way, well pleased with the novel and uncommon incident of making and using snow-balls in summer.

At Work in the "Flume."

I went one day with a gang of workmen to repair the bridge over the Pemigewasset River, and the footways by which visitors reach the "Flume." The storms and freshets of winter always do more or less damage to the bridges, foot-paths, plank-walks, and other contrivances for the convenience, comfort and safety of the summer visitors, which are not removed at the close of the travelling season.

I will try to give those who have not seen it some idea of this great natural curiosity.

The " Flume " is reached from the bridge across the river, by a foot-path which follows the course of the stream, crossing it often, leading up and over steep rocks, and sometimes following the bed of the stream itself. At every step something is seen to admire.

The stream pours itself through the " Flume " over an inclined plane of smooth, polished rock, six hundred feet in length, and very gradual in descent. Precipices from sixty to eighty feet high wall in the waters on each side ; the space between them averages about twenty feet, except at the upper end, where the walls suddenly approach each other within ten feet, and hold suspended between them, in mid-air, an enormous boulder of granite, which looks as if a very small force would send it into the stream below, so slight appears its hold between the cliffs. The precipices on each side are fringed with tall forest-trees, and the sun shines into the ravine only about two hours a day. It is at all times a grand and gloomy scene. The only way to get up this narrow gorge is by a foot-way of planks and logs which is kept in repair by the proprietors.

A huge tree has fallen across from one side to the other, above the boulder, and many persons have crossed the ravine on it. It is a dizzy height, and the foothold is not very secure, the log being rotten and slippery.

Having repaired the bridge, we proceeded to the " Flume " to fix up the foot-ways. We there found an army of small black flies, or midges, as they are called. These troublesome little insects, which are far worse than mosquitoes, abound in the woods and all over the mountains, and annoy every one with merciless perseverance. They seldom show themselves in the houses, and will keep away from a person who is smoking. All workmen outside are obliged to make a fire and keep up a smoke, in order to be able to work. We built a huge fire at one end of the " Flume," and thus kept the flies away ; a gust of wind would sometimes drive so much smoke in upon us as to compel us to drop our tools, and run out to avoid suffocation. This hindered us a good deal, but we preferred to be smoked out occasionally rather than to bear the constant torment of the flies.

The logs on which the plank foot-ways of the previous summer had rested having been washed away, it was necessary for us to cut down some trees for new ones ; in order to procure what we needed, we ascended a narrow path to the top of one side of the ravine, and, cutting down the trees, we trimmed them and rolled them over the brink into the chasm below.

Looking over to the opposite side of the ravine, I saw a tall tree standing on the edge of the precipice, and determined to go across and fell it ; I wished to see it fall into the " Flume " with all its branches on. Taking my axe, I started over the log I have spoken of as lying across the chasm; I had nearly reached the other side when my foot struck a projecting knot, I lost my balance, and what saved me from falling was a desperate spring, and my grasp on a bush which grew near the edge. I was startled, and it was some time before I could go to work; at last I began to cut down the tree, which soon began to reel, and the breeze taking it on the right side, it slowly inclined in the desired direction; I ran to a safe distance, and leaned over the edge as far as I dared, with one hand grasping the branch of a tree, to see it fall. It went down head-foremost, and was, to my surprise, considerably shorter than the depth of the ravine; it struck on its head, stood upright for an instant, as if surprised at its novel situation, and then its heavy butt-end went down on the bed of the stream with a crash like that of a thousand thunders. The earth shook and trembled beneath my feet, and the sensations I then experienced will never be forgotten.

I felled two more trees, but not with the same success, and, we having enough for the footways, I looked about for a way to the bottom of the ravine. The log by which I had crossed was still open to me, and a path was on the other side; but as I did not wish to trust the log again, I finally scrambled down the steep side of the precipice, and reached the bottom with only a few trifling bruises and scratches. We were obliged to work, much of the time, in three or four feet of water, which was cold as ice, and were very glad when the job was finished.

Almost an Accident.

Early on the morning of the Fourth of July, the mulatto hostler of the Profile House brought a small cannon, or swivel, into the front yard. It had been used, the previous summer, for the entertainment of the guests who wished to hear the echoes waked by its discharge on the shore of Echo Lake, and had become rusty by long exposure to the weather. The mulatto filled the cannon nearly full of fine sporting gunpowder, grass and dirt, rammed it down as hard as possible, and then, lighting a match, attempted to discharge it; failing to do so, he gave it up for the present, and left the cannon in the yard.

Another man came along, discovered how the cannon was loaded, and removed it to the back side of the hotel. Having reached a distance which he considered safe, he inserted a fuse in the priming, lit it, and ran away. The cannon burst; and a piece of iron weighing twenty pounds went over the Profile House and buried itself in the front yard, less than four feet from one of the guests who was walking there. It was very fortunate that the mulatto did not succeed in discharging the cannon; he would have been torn in pieces, and much other damage would have been done.

My First Visit to the "Old Man."

About the last of July I determined to pay a visit to the head of the "Old Man." While getting ready for the attempt, I thought, if I got there, I would set up a pole and raise a flag; I also concluded to remain on the top of the Mountain until after dark, and then build a large bonfire. I procured a hatchet, which I always thereafter carried in my belt in all my wanderings, a flag ten feet long and five feet wide, a long cord, a bag of shavings, and kindling-wood and some provisions; altogether they made a heavy load to carry to the top of the Mountain, a mile and a half, on a hot day in summer.

At one o'clock, P. M., I left the Profile House, and commenced the ascent of Cannon Mountain, so called from there being, near its top, a rock, which, seen from a certain point, resembles a cannon mounted on a carriage; it is also called Profile Mountain, as it is on its side that the "Old Man" is situated.

I followed the footpath, and found it very hard work to get along with my load, but reached the top, and deposited it in a convenient place for use at the proper time. After resting a little, I began to descend toward the "Old Man," which lies about a mile away in an opposite direction from that in which I ascended. The way was far more difficult than I had supposed; huge rocks were scattered around, among and over which I had to carefully choose my way. Long before I saw any signs of the "Old Man," I was much inclined to give it up; but I remembered that some one had been on the Head before, and that "what man has done, man may do."

I might not be, and probably was not, following the route taken by the other party, but any way to the Head must be hard and dangerous; so I pushed on, and was finally rewarded, as I supposed, by arriving at the spot I wished to find. Looking about for a flag-staff, I saw that the nearest wood was half a mile farther down, and that much of the way to it lay along the brink of a frightful precipice. The descent required great care; for in some places a slip of the foot would send me to be dashed in pieces on the rocks more than a thousand feet below, and a false step anywhere would be a serious thing. I finally reached the wood, and selected a fine stick, fifteen feet long, and five inches in diameter at the larger end, which I trimmed with my hatchet, and succeeded, after immense labor, in transporting to what seemed to be the right place.

From the spot where I stood I could see the lake at the foot of the Mountain, and many people on the shore. I had told no one of my in-

tentions when I left the hotel, and now began to regret it, as, if anything prevented me from getting back, nobody would know where to look
for me, and the consequences might not be pleasant. However, by getting on a large rock and waving the flag, I attracted the attention of the
people, who waved hats and handkerchiefs to show that they saw me.
I now felt easier in my mind, as, if I was missed, my location would
readily be inferred.

Raising the pole, I placed it in a cleft in a rock, piling large stones
around it to secure it, and then flung the flag to the breeze.

I saw it was getting late, and I made the best of my way back to
the place where I had left my load. The descent was hard, as I have
said, but the return was worse, and I was nearly exhausted before reaching the top. Selecting a good place near the " Cannon," I spent the
next two hours in collecting wood, brush, and green spruce-trees ; at the
end of that time I had a very large pile, under which I arranged the
kindlings, and sat down to wait for the proper time to set the pile on fire.
I determined to wait until nine o'clock, because many of the guests would
then be in the piazza of the hotel, and also because the stages usually
arrived about that time. It now occurred to me that I had not taken
time to consider the enterprise carefully, in all its bearings, before starting.

There was no moon ; I had omitted to bring a lantern, and I might
find it difficult to get back, if I was obliged to stay out all night. To
miss the path would be dangerous in the extreme, and to keep it in the
darkness would be difficult. I might meet with the same mishap as that
which happened in the year 1859 to Charles Barrett, a wealthy deaf-
mute of Boston, now dead. He was one of a party of deaf-mutes who
had been attending a Convention in Vermont, and were now visiting the
Profile House. Most of them had made the ascent of Mount Lafayette,
and they were seated around the fire after supper, enjoying themselves,
when one of them suddenly asked what became of Mr. Barrett, who had
not accompanied them up the Mountain. None of them had seen him
since their return. Investigation proved that he was not about the
hotel, but one of the servants remembered having seen him going up
the path leading to the top of Cannon Mountain, and that he was alone.
This caused instant alarm, and men were despatched up the Mountain,
with lanterns, to hunt for him. As the search progressed, his hat, cravat,
coat, etc., were found in various places. He was finally found far out
of the regular path, wandering aimlessly and distractedly about, and
most completely lost. Before him, and directly in his way, was a steep
precipice, and in all probability a few minutes' delay would have proved
fatal. When he found that he was saved, his strength, which was nearly
exhausted, gave way entirely, and he became unconscious. It was necessary to carry him most of the way back to the hotel, where a liberal
use of restoratives soon put him all right.

Having thought it all over, I concluded to carry out my original plan, and proceeded to eat my luncheon as a beginning. The wind in this elevated spot blew quite hard, and I felt chilly, as my clothing was damp with perspiration. Finding a cleft in a rock which would protect me from the wind, I crept into it and remained two hours; the large bag in which I had brought the shavings served me as a shawl, and I was quite comfortable in body, although still somewhat uneasy in mind about getting down.

All was utter silence around me; the rapidly-increasing darkness, and the distance back, were not pleasant subjects for thought.

I was indeed, for the time, " monarch of all I surveyed "; but if my realm was limited by my vision, it was small indeed, and my crown by no means sat lightly on my brow. My watch finally told me, by the aid of a match, that it was nine o'clock, and I fired the pile; the wind fanned the flame to a huge blaze thirty feet or more in height, which illuminated the scene for miles around, and was quickly seen from the hotel. They told me afterwards that a cry of " fire " was raised, and every one of the three hundred and fifty persons then at the hotel was outside in a very few minutes, and enjoyed the scene very much. In about half an hour the fire died away; as soon as my eyes, which had been blinded by the blaze, became accustomed to the darkness, I set out to return; I could barely see to keep the path, and stumbled and fell quite often.

After a long and tedious journey, I arrived at the Profile House with no other damage than a bruised knee. The next morning inquiry was made about the fire, and a desire was expressed to see the person who made it; I was sent for and presented to the company, who, on being acquainted with the facts, made up a handsome contribution for me. The contribution was very welcome, I am free to say; but I do not think that I would do the same job over again for the same amount. A man will sometimes do a thing for his own gratification which he cannot afterward be hired to do at any price.

Going down to the lake, I was surprised to find that the pole was not on the Head, but some distance from it, among a group of rocks called " Adam's Apples." Not content to leave the job half done, I jumped into a boat, rowed across the lake, and struck off and up through the pathless woods to the pole, which I planted in another place. The Head was a very difficult and dangerous place to move or stand on. Returning to the lake, I found that the pole was in the right place.

In a few days, work was discontinued on the hotel, as the proprietors were obliged to give all their time to the rapidly-increasing number of guests, and I was dismissed, with orders to return after the travelling season was over. And so ended my first summer at the Mountains.

SECOND SUMMER.

IN GENERAL.

THE travelling season at the Mountains begins about the last of June or by the middle of July, and ends in September, or early in October. While at home, during the summer or fall, waiting the close of the travelling season, that I might return to the Mountains and watch the approach of winter, I laid my plans, and provided things which experience and observation had taught me were necessary in mountain wanderings: strong clothing, not easily torn by bushes and briars, through which I might have to force my way; a knapsack, drinking-flask, hand-axe, etc. I rejected the idea of a gun, as being both inconvenient and unnecessary. An axe, I thought, would serve all ordinary purposes of offence and defence, and in case of the appearance of a bear or other large animal, I could run away. My grandfather—a deaf-mute—used only to carry a hay-fork when he went after his cows, at a time when wild beasts were plenty; and he said he found it a very efficient weapon.

Orders at last came for me to return and resume work at the Profile House, and I accordingly departed for the Mountains, where, on my arrival, I received a hearty welcome.

The first thing I did after arriving there, was to hurry down to the spot from which the "Profile" can best be seen, and take a good look at my old friend, whose towering form loomed up in the gathering darkness like some grim sentinel standing guard over the forest. Having paid my respects to him, I returned to the hotel, of which I will give a brief description:

It has four hundred windows, and can accommodate several hundred guests. It is built in the form of a cross, and stands on a level plain, a few acres in extent, surrounded on all sides by lofty mountains. Its front faces the Franconia Notch, through which the waters of the Echo and Profile Lakes flow into the Pemigewasset River, and thence into Lake Winnipisoegee. It is one of the most convenient, commodious, and best-managed hotels in the Mountains; it is within easy distance of some of the most interesting of the natural curiosities: Eagle Cliff, Echo and Profile Lakes, the Cascade and Falls, the "Old Man," the Basin, Pool, and Flume, Walker's Falls, and other minor objects. With its telegraph and stage offices, its hosts of servants and hundreds of guests, it is a town in itself. Immense quantities of provisions are consumed, and teams are constantly bringing the necessaries and luxuries of life over the Mountains from Littleton, eleven miles off. The establishment is supplied with pure mountain spring water, than which the world knows no better article. The stables are extensive, as the travel

About three-fourths of a mile from the Profile House, nestling among the hills, and surrounded by a dense growth of trees, lies Echo Lake, a beautiful sheet of water, from which can be seen Eagle Cliff, Cannon Mountain, and Bald Mountain. It is remarkable for its echoes; the blowing of a tin horn, or shouting with the voice, will awake the " babbling gossips of the air," who will return the sounds with wonderful distinctness; the report of a swivel or gun fired in a certain direction, will reverberate like peals of thunder among the Mountains. All this I know only from hearsay, and waking the echoes is one of the few occasions on which I keenly feel my loss of hearing. The best time to visit the lake is near sunset,—the magical beauty of the scene can then be best understood; and, if a man be in a meditative mood, there is no better place to " look through nature up to nature's God."

Take a boat, and row to the middle of the lake, which is about one mile long and three-quarters of a mile wide, and of great depth and clearness, and, by looking down into the water, you can readily imagine yourself floating in mid-air.

I have twice stolen out at midnight, and paddled around the lake by moonlight. On one occasion, the report having spread that a bear and a deer had been seen at the farther end of the lake, my curiosity induced me to take a boat and go down to the place by moonlight, to see if anything was to be seen. Arriving there, I stepped on shore, advanced a few steps, and peered into the bushes. I could see nothing; and the perfect stillness around me, together with the strange hour, gave me a sudden panic, and I dashed into the boat and swept homeward with all possible speed.

The lake is a very popular resort, and parties often carry musical instruments out in the boats, the playing of which has a very fine effect. It is one of those places of which the more you see the more you wish to see.

Eagle Cliff.

On the left of the Profile House is Eagle Cliff, a huge columnar crag, which towers far into the air, and seems almost to overhang the hotel, although it is in reality quite a distance off. Its top is a huge mass of jagged rocks, which leans over so much that it seems ready to fall from its place. The cliff derives its name from the fact that, high up on its face, and plainly visible from the hotel, there is a black-looking hole.

where, for many years, a pair of eagles built their nest. Some mischievous persons went up one summer, with fire-arms, and frightened them away, much to the grief and indignation of the visitors, to whom the noble birds had afforded much gratification.

I have several times seen eagles sailing about the spot, and occasionally diving into the woods and then soaring away. I could not, from the distance, ascertain whether they obtained any prey, but was much interested in their movements, and wished for a nearer view. One day I was watching an eagle who had been hovering about the spot for some days, when I determined to get nearer, if possible. I plunged into the woods, and made my way as directly as I could towards the cliff. Reaching its foot, I commenced climbing up, taking care to keep out of sight of the eagle, who was now directly above me, sailing in a circle. I reached the foot of the crag, a distance of about three-quarters of a mile, after much exertion, and halted to rest. Through the branches above me I saw that the eagle had gone up higher, and I was afraid I had frightened him away. Wishing to get a better position, I crept cautiously on my hands and knees, and had nearly arrived at the place I wished, when I saw a plump rabbit sitting near its burrow. I sat down and watched it. In a few minutes I saw a dark object drop rapidly from the sky; the rabbit disappeared in its burrow; and the baffled eagle, for it was he, paused a moment, as if considering the situation, and then spreading his broad wings, he soared aloft again. He was only a short distance from me, and I had a splendid view of him. He was a noble specimen of the king of birds, with broad wings, heavy beak, and powerful claws. A momentary wish for a gun crossed my mind, but the next minute I was ashamed of myself, for it seemed almost a crime to shoot such a bird.

In about five minutes the rabbit appeared again, and almost at the same instant the eagle swept down, with a speed which set the bushes and leaves in motion like a breeze; and, grasping the unlucky rabbit in its claws, sailed gracefully away over the forest, and disappeared behind the cliff.

Before leaving the spot I took a survey of the rocks at the foot of the crag, and in one place I noticed a huge slab of rock standing on its edge, with a very slight hold on the face of the cliff. It had been loosened by frost, or other causes, and was evidently ready to slip or slide down the mountain by a very slight force. It would, I think, cover a quarter of an acre, and certainly weighed many tons.

The next spring, before the snow had quite disappeared, I was one day going to dinner with the rest of the workmen, when I suddenly felt a heavy jarring of the earth beneath my feet. At the same instant the man behind me gave me a heavy blow on the back, and when I turned sharply around, pointed to Eagle Cliff. I looked, and saw that the great slab before mentioned had got loose, and gone crashing and tearing to the foot of the Mountain. Deaf though I was, I was sensible of a terrible crash and an indescribable roaring. An immense column of smoke rose slowly up, and gradually disappeared.

The next morning I was one of a party who ascended to the spot where the slab had been. The immense mass of rock had cleared a path for itself for many rods below, sweeping the trees before it like chaff, and grinding some of them to powder. Rocks, large and small, were scattered far and wide, as they had been hurled from the path of the slab in its passage downward. I have seen snow-avalanches sweep down a mountain-side, and carry much before them, but this, being a solid mass of rock, far exceeded them in destructive force. I am inclined to think a number of such slides, at different periods, are what caused the outline of a human face known as "The Old Man," and I also think that, in time, other slides will occur which will entirely obliterate it. In my explorations over and upon the rocks which constitute the "Profile," I have noticed crevices and cracks in abundance, on which the action of frost and ice must eventually have a ruinous result. Of this I shall speak more fully hereafter, and shall also have more to say of Eagle Cliff, with which I afterwards became intimately acquainted.

Building a Boat-House.

A boat-house being required at the Profile Lake, I was selected to build it. It was by no means a pleasant job, not on account of the work—that was easy enough—but by reason of the spot being just within the woods, which close down on the lake and swarm with midgets. These pests of the mountains often shorten the visits of tourists; they especially interfere with the labors of the artists, the enjoyment of the ramblers, and peace of everybody, everywhere, except in the hotels, their immediate vicinity, and some few other favored spots. I commenced operations, keeping up a fire to windward, and working in the smoke as best I might. From the spot where I worked I had a full view of the "Old Man," and, during the month that I was stationed there, I saw him in all the various aspects which the changes in the weather give him. My attention was divided between my work and the "Old Man" a good part of the time, and I often hit my fingers in the attempt to drive a nail and look the other way at once. Somehow, I could not help looking; the stern old face had a sort of fascination for me, and I almost worshipped it sometimes. Working at the lake, I had charge of the boats used by the guests of the hotel. One day I saw a stout old gentleman and three ladies coming towards the boats.

They stopped to enjoy the scenery for some time, and then the old gentleman called for me. I had my eyes on him, expecting to be spoken to, and I pointed to my ears and shook my head. He pointed to the boat, with a smile, and then to himself and party, signifying that he wanted one. I came down and cast one off for him; he stepped into it, stood erect, while the ladies took seats, and then throwing off his coat and gloves, he sat down, put out the oars, and sent the boat over the surface of the lake with a long, regular stroke, which showed him to be a sailor, and a man-of-war. In the course of an hour he returned, paid the customary fee, and went away. His bearing convinced me that he was no ordinary man. There were no signs of rank about him, only an indefinable something which created that impression. In the evening there was a ball, and I saw the old gentleman walking about with quite a crowd following, and learned that he was Admiral Farragut. I mentally did homage to the naval hero, and studied him with interest, during his stay in the grand parlor where the ball took place. The next day, while I was at work as usual, the Admiral came along, asked for slate and pencil, and engaged me in conversation in regard to the circumstances attending my visit to the "Old Man," while I was constructing my "model"; a copy of which, hanging in the hotel, had attracted his attention on the previous evening. In regard to my exploration on the dizzy heights of the "Profile," the Admiral asked me if I was not afraid at the time; to which, Yankee-like, I replied by asking him if he was not afraid when he stood in the shrouds of his vessel at the capture of New Orleans? He incidentally remarked that he was acquainted with the veteran Laurent Clerc, who came from France, the first instructor of deaf-mutes in America, and others of our notable men.

At the close of the interview I felt much elated by having had a personal conversation, all to myself, with the hero of New Orleans. There was nothing remarkable, to be sure, in his talking with me as he did; but in my regard to the fact as one of the events of my life, I am no more absurd, to say the least, than are the multitudes who throng wherever our great statesmen and generals happen to sojourn, and crowd and elbow each other in desperate eagerness to get a sight of the man or a shake of his hand. The Admiral impressed me as a dignified, but genial old man, with nothing of the aristocrat about him—a genuine son of the sea—fond of society, and carrying with him a certain air, which, while conducive to social intercourse, repelled any approach to familiarity. I hoped to see him again, but when I returned from my work at night, I learned that he was gone. I saw him, some time afterward, in the Railroad Station, at Hartford, Conn., and had the pleasure of being recognized, and getting a shake of his hand, just as he stepped on board of a train. He stands high in my estimation of men, and, hero-worship or not, I say: Long live Admiral Farragut.

A Week with a Photographer.

There came to the Profile House a seedy-looking man, whose baggage was two heavy chests, and who, as we soon discovered, was a photographer, sent by a firm in New York to take views of the places of interest in the Mountains. He was not a very prepossessing individual; wore an army uniform, and had only one eye, black and piercing, but we were soon interested in him. We learned that he went out with Dr. Kane's expedition in search of Sir John Franklin, as a photographer, but the intense cold prevented him from taking views, and he was otherwise employed. He had been in the army during our civil war, and a splinter destroyed one of his eyes at the battle of Malvern Hill.

He had come to the Mountains at the wrong time, July and August being the best months for photographing. He remained over a week without seeing a single fair day, and was almost in despair. He wished to engage me to guide and assist him in taking views, at the first opportunity, and I obtained permission to help him for a week. He wished to go to some parts of the Mountains which had never been visited by photographers.

We loaded ourselves with his apparatus and other necessary articles, and went here and there for some time with varied success. He at last decided to ascend Eagle Cliff, and try to get views of the Profile House and the surrounding scenery. Our loads weighed over a hundred pounds each, and the ascent was hard indeed, but we finally reached the spot where I had watched the eagle, as related before. We cut down several trees, made a clearing, and built a staging about six feet high, from which a wide view could be had. He succeeded in taking several good pictures.

The next day we talked it over, and determined to camp out two days. Taking our loads, as before, with provisions enough to last until our return, we proceeded to the "Basin," taking views on the way.

The "Basin" is a deep hollow worn in the solid granite by the long-continued action of the water, which falls into it over a ledge a few feet in height, and escapes through a small opening at the opposite side. Its shortest width is twenty feet, and its depth fifteen feet. It forms a mammoth bowl, which is always filled with very cold and pure water. The water is very clear, and the bottom can be distinctly seen. Viewed from a certain spot on one side, the other side assumes the form of a gigantic foot, with the sole outward, and fully exposed to the action of the water. It is a beautiful place, close to the road, and it is pleasant to linger there and watch the eddying whirl of waters.

At the Basin we determined to remain all day and night. After taking a few views in different positions, in each of which I figured, the photographer removed his apparatus to the other side, and had got it adjusted, when he hit one leg of the stand with his foot and sent the whole into the Basin. In trying to save it, he slipped, and fell in himself. I was standing near him, and, knowing that he could not swim, I made such haste to catch him that I, too, went headlong into the water. The water was icy cold, it being near November. Being a good swimmer, I soon placed my companion where he could hold on for a few minutes, and having got out myself, I helped him to do the same. We were in a bad way, certainly; both of us wet to the skin, and the apparatus fifteen feet under water. The poor fellow actually wept, believing he had lost it forever; but I told him I would get it again, even if I had to dive for it. Procuring a long pole, we made a very good grappling with some nails we had with us, and let it down, but found it too short. Splicing it with cords, we again let it down, and, as I was feeling about for the object of our search, I lost my balance and fell into the Basin a second time. I had, at previous times, like many others, stood on the brink of the Basin, and longed for a plunge in the " delicious-looking bath"; but I changed my mind entirely after this second experience, and at all subsequent visits to the spot, I " looked but longed no more." Undaunted, I climbed out, and we renewed our attempts to recover the apparatus, which we finally succeeded in doing.

Oh! how we capered and laughed, forgetting that we were thoroughly wet, two miles from any house, and without the means to make a fire. By the time that we began to realize our situation, and consider what we should do, a team happened along and we procured some matches of the driver, and determined to stay all night, as we had at first intended. We built a large fire, and so far dried our clothes that we felt comfortable, and then worked on till near sundown, when we looked about for a place to spend the night. I remembered having seen a small shanty, somewhere in the vicinity, a year before, and went to look for it. After a diligent search, I found it about half a mile away, and returned to guide my comrade to it, marking the trees as I went, to insure a speedy return. It was the best place we could find; and we proceeded to make ourselves comfortable, although the fact that there was an old bear-trap near by, brought up rather unpleasant associations; the idea of one of those animals coming along, not being agreeable.

We ate our supper cold, and made our bed with moss and blankets. We were afraid to build a fire in that place, for fear of a conflagration in the woods, a thing which had happened before from the same cause. The gloom of the forest, and the rapidly-increasing darkness, were indeed thrilling. The darkness put it out of our power to converse, which was rather uncomfortable. All was utter silence to me; my companion doing the hearing for both of us, while, I suppose, I did my share of the thinking. Neither of us slept much that night, the strangeness of my position and my own thoughts keeping me awake; while the rustling of swaying branches, the voice of falling waters, and the hooting of owls, made it impossible for him to sleep. He told me afterward, that the owls scared him badly; and I confessed that my imagination conjured up so many bears, snakes, and other denizens of the forest, that I was heartily glad when morning came. At day-break my companion fell asleep, and remained so, until a large owl, of which I had a good view, awakened him by its hooting, when I told him to keep watch, and was soon asleep, careless whether he obeyed orders or not.

Refreshed by our naps, we ate our breakfasts and returned to the Basin, from which we went to the Pool, but were unable to take any views, on account of cloudy weather. We took lodgings at the Flume House, and the next day, after obtaining views of the Flume, we commenced our return.

Arriving at the foot of Mount Lafayette, we halted, and held a consultation as to the possible advantage of ascending it, and the probability of being able to obtain views from its summit. It was late in the season, and the ascent was dangerous, on account of the frost-clouds, to be caught in one of which is almost certain death.

I had ventured up, a few days before, at a time when there was a dense frost-cloud, and all the trees above were covered with a white and glistening coat of frost. I wanted to *feel* how cold it was, and to ascertain how far I could endure it. (The reader will observe, that to go up when a frost-cloud is abroad, and approach it from below, is a very different thing from having one sweep down upon, and envelope, the unfortunate person who happens to be in the way. In the former case, one can retreat at pleasure; in the latter, one seldom escapes with life.) I carried with me overcoat and mittens, which I did not need to put on for some time, it being a warm day. As I approached the border of the frost-cloud, I put them on, and ventured some distance up. I *felt* it, sure enough. It was a stinging, suffocating cold; the air was filled with minute particles of frozen mist, and my hair and beard were quickly white; while my clothes, before I left, were frozen stiff. When I could bear the cold no longer, I beat a retreat.

I noticed a very singular thing during my stay: The wind was blowing quite hard, and the particles of mist or frost, clinging to the trees and to each other, made icicles, which did not hang down as we generally see them, but stood out horizontally from trees, rocks, stumps, etc., giving the whole a very striking appearance.

As I descended to warmer regions, the heat gradually thawed out my frozen clothes; and when I arrived at the foot of the mountain, I was as wet as if I had been plunged under water. It will now be seen how dangerous it was for us to venture up. If we reached the top, and a frost-cloud should be seen coming, we could not possibly reach a place of safety with our loads. We finally decided to make the attempt.

The photographer and myself slowly ascended with our heavy loads, keeping a sharp look-out, after leaving the line of the forest, for any appearance of danger. As we neared the top of the Mountain we saw a spot of cloud afar off, which I knew was a sign of the approach of the frost-demon, and we turned and rapidly made our way back, narrowly escaping the deadly embraces of the cloud, so speedily did it sweep after us. Of course, all our labor was lost; taking views was impossible. We gave up the attempt, and returned to the Profile House. The next day we made an equally fruitless ascent of Cannon Mountain; after which, the prospect was so bad that my photographing friend gave up the job, packed his things, bade farewell to the Mountains, and returned to New York.

A Deaf and Dumb Guide better than None.

Soon after the departure of my friend the one-eyed photograph man, a gentleman made his appearance at the Profile House, who hailed from New Jersey. He came very late, as the season had closed to all intents and purposes, and only a few stragglers remained of the swarm of visitors. He inquired for a Guide, and was told that the regular Guides had all gone home, but that I would make a good one, as I was well acquainted with the Mountains, and had served in that capacity before. On learning that I was deaf and dumb, he flatly refused to take me, adding some very uncomplimentary remarks, which were reported to me, of which I took no apparent notice, although I made a memorandum of them in my mind. One day he ventured out alone, in search of Walker's Falls, of which I shall have more to say hereafter. It was in the afternoon, and the hill-tops were enveloped in clouds. The distance to the Falls, from the road leading to the Flume House, is one mile and a-half. Neglect and mountain storms had nearly obliterated that half of the path nearest the Falls, making it easy to lose one's way. At sundown, the gentleman had not returned, and an alarm was raised. I was requested to go in search of him, and at once consented, glad of the chance to show him that his estimation of a Deaf and Dumb was wrong; and I started off alone. After leaving the road, I soon found his trail in the soft moss, it retaining the impression of a person's foot for a long time, and pursued it with all possible haste, as the dusk was coming on and time was precious.

It was necessary for me to keep directly on the trail, and I, being deaf, might pass quite near him without seeing him, and he might not see or hear me. I found, by the direction of his trail, that he had gone wrong, and could not possibly have reached the Falls. I found him perched on a rock, wiping his brow vigorously. He had given himself up for lost, and his conduct, when he saw me, somewhat belied his previously-expressed opini... of a deaf-mute guide. He caught my hand and shook it warmly. We had no time to waste in words, and if we had, it was too dark to write, by which method only could we communicate.

Beckoning him to follow, I took the back track, and went forward at a rapid rate, up hill and down, over rocks and stumps, through bushes and briars, intent on gaining the main road before utter darkness came on. He came after me, panting and perspiring, frequently stumbling over some obstacles, and falling headlong; and, plainly objecting to such rapid locomotion. I confess to having experienced a sort of malicious pleasure in leading him such a race, in consideration of his remarks on me the other day. After a while I became slightly anxious, as the darkness increased, lest we should miss the way; but while turning it over in my mind, we burst through a clump of bushes, directly into the road, and I shortly had the pleasure of seeing him safe in the arms of his anxious wife.

For the rest of his stay, he employed me as his guide, paying me liberally; besides stating, at the close of my engagement, that, although he had travelled much, both in the old world and the new, he had never had a better guide.

My Ascent of Mount Lafayette.

The most remarkable sight I had ever witnessed, occurred one afternoon this season. The clouds were gathering, and slowly descending, and there was every appearance of a rain-storm, when I determined to venture up the Mountain, to see whether it was clear at the top. I hurried up as fast as I could, and having made the ascent, passing through a dense cloud on my way, I was rewarded by a singular sight. Below me, and shutting off all other view, was, apparently, a thick field of cotton, almost tempting me to jump into its soft folds. I learned afterward, that soon after my departure from the hotel it commenced raining heavily, and the people there thought I was in a bad plight for venturing on the Mountain at such an improper time. They did not appreciate my love of adventure, and my desire to experience the sensation of being above a storm-cloud. I had often read of persons standing on the top of a mountain while there was a storm raging below them, and I now felt quite elated at my good fortune in witnessing a similar scene.

Very soon the cotton-cloud changed to a bright red color, as if on fire, caught from the sun, which was shining brightly above. The scene now became sublime, beyond my ability to describe. I was reminded of the Israelites fleeing from Egypt, guided by a pillar of fire by night. For many miles around, this magnificent sight met my eye. Soon, however, I noticed that the cloud was rising, which made me feel quite uneasy, for fear that I should get a thorough soaking, which would render me quite uncomfortable, and perhaps place me in a dangerous plight from the cold and wet, and there was no chance for escape; so I had to content myself by waiting its approach. I saw no lightning, nor did I feel any jar from the thunder, in which I was somewhat disappointed. As the cloud arose, I was agreeably surprised to find that it did not rain at all, but there was a thick mist or cloud rising fast, and in a few minutes it had passed above my head, slowly uniting, until it appeared like a great white cloth or sheet spread over many miles around. The whole Mountain range came into full view, in all its grandeur and majesty.

I was riveted to the spot in amazement at this unexpected scene, and I can hardly find words to portray the beautiful spectacle. The rising of a mammoth curtain in a mammoth theatre, might give some idea of what I beheld coming into view: a grand panorama of splendid and varied landscape. Mount Washington, thirty miles away, revealed itself in mighty grandeur, with all its surroundings of minor hills. But the descending sun warned me not to tarry, but to hasten down while yet there was daylight enough to guide my steps. I found most of the path very wet and muddy, but reached the hotel without harm.

A Party Overwhelmed by a Severe Rain-Storm.

To show the danger there is in incautiously attempting an ascent of the Mountains, I will narrate an incident that occurred in the early part of this season.

A party of five gentlemen and five ladies determined to risk the ascent of Mount Lafayette quite early, being, I think, the first party of the season, notwithstanding the remonstrances of the hotel-keeper. The weather appeared quite unpromising, but, having a guide, they ventured off, and reached the top of the Mountain without particular adventure. They had hardly dismounted, and taken a view of the scene before them, when they were surrounded by a dense cloud, which totally obscured their vision. Quickly mounting their horses, they had gone but a few rods when a heavy rain-storm burst upon them, forming a torrent, which filled the path so that they could not find their way.

The horses refused to move, being frightened and bewildered, and even a hard beating had no effect upon them. The whole party was in a very dangerous plight, for they were pitiable-looking objects, completely drenched; and the ladies looked most miserable, helpless, and trembling with fear and the cold. They were held on to the horses by the gentlemen accompanying them, or they would have fallen exhausted to the ground. The rain poured in ceaseless torrents, as if from sheer malice, to punish the imprudent adventurers.

There was great consternation at the hotel when the storm came on, as it seemed unlikely that any of the party could survive its chilling effects. A quick consultation was had, and volunteers called for to go to the rescue. I quickly offered my services; and six others following my example, we hastily procured a two-horse carriage, and drove with great speed the three miles to the foot of the Mountain. Here we unharnessed the horses from the carriage, tying them, so they should not stray, and proceeded on foot up the Mountain, which we did with great difficulty, discomfort, and danger, the path being filled with water, and the pelting rain nearly blinding us. Finally, we reached the spot where the party stood, more dead than alive, and truly pitiable objects to behold. We did not stop to ask any questions, but quickly got the ladies off the horses, gave them a drink of something which the strictest teetotaller would probably not have denied them under the circumstances, and then each took one of the ladies and started down the Mountain again, the gentlemen gladly following with all possible speed. The horses were also induced to move, and when we got half way down, and had partially revived the almost perishing party, we again mounted them on their horses, putting a man on each side to hold them in place. By dint of great caution, we finally reached the carriage, into which we placed the ladies, letting their horses gallop off towards home. Again harnessing our horses to the carriage, we started off with all speed to the hotel, where we arrived without further mishap. The travelling party received prompt aid and by careful nursing, and the use of proper stimulants, they were fortunately able to be about the next morning, apparently none the worse for their dangerous predicament.

The Adventurous Little Girl.

One Sunday afternoon, a little waiter-girl, not more than eleven years old, banteringly said that she would ascend Mount Lafayette alone, if no one would accompany her. Some of the older boys, who were fond of mischief, wishing to see some fun, and to test her strength, offered to go with her, promising help, if necessary, in the ascent and descent.

So off they started to the foot of the Mountain, without the knowledge of any older persons. The ascent was very difficult for one so young: she started up very courageously, but her strength not being equal to the task, she soon faltered; but the boys cruelly drove her up, by threats. She often wavered, but finally was enabled to nearly reach the top, a distance of about three miles from the foot of the Mountain. Here her tired limbs refused any longer to sustain her, and she fell, exhausted, to the ground.

The boys became quite alarmed at this result of their persuasion and threats, and, finding that the sun was getting well down, they became frightened, for fear that they should all perish with the cold at night. One of the oldest, more courageous than the rest, offered to stay with the little girl while the rest should hasten back for help. Arriving at the hotel, they quickly gave the alarm, and men were despatched for the little adventurer. She was brought down the Mountain more dead than alive, having fearful spasms, and reached the hotel utterly exhausted. A messenger was sent five miles for a doctor, by whose care she was revived, but without any particular desire to try such a jaunt again. It is, perhaps, needless to say, that the boys were more careful afterward, heartily thankful that no ill effects followed their fool-hardiness.

Taking the Measure of the Old Man of the Mountain.

One day, while looking at the stucco-workers at the hotel, the idea struck me that a *fac-simile* of the "Old Man of the Mountain" might be made of Calcined Plaster. This *was* an idea which promised large rewards if it could be accomplished. But how to get an exact counterfeit presentment of His High Mightiness, *that* was the question. Cheered with the hope of success, I soon had my wits at work determining how to get at the measurements of the various rocks which combine to make up this wonderful profile. I was satisfied that it would take many weary hours of toil and danger to accomplish the task I had laid out for myself, but I was determined to succeed, and *I did.*

Preparing a clothes-line forty feet long, and a piece of white cotton cloth about four feet square, to the top and bottom of which I fastened heavy pieces of wood, so that their weight should keep the cloth smooth when spread out and suspended. One morning, without informing any one of my intention, I started quite early, taking along the line and cloth, not forgetting a lunch, and my little hatchet, and made the ascent directly from the Bowling Alley, straight to the Face, instead of by the ordinary path. The ascent was very difficult and dangerous, and I was very much fatigued, but finally succeeded in gaining the top.

After careful examination below, I reached the top of the head, and having attached my cloth to the line, I lowered it over the face, and fastened it in a crack in the rock. I could not see where it ended; so, after partaking of my lunch, I started back down the Mountain, being obliged to go to a point eighty rods beyond the hotel, in order to see where the cloth had rested. I found that it had landed on the nose, and, as that was one-half the height of the whole profile, I knew that the entire height must be *eighty feet,* or twice the length of my forty-foot line.

While I was still looking up at the face, some one gave the alarm at the hotel, that some vandal had painted a white spot on the Old Man's nose, and quite spoiled his beauty. The hotel keeper sent his clerk to ascertain what had been done, and to stop further depredations. Finding me intently watching the head, he presumed at once that I was the mischief-maker; he shook his fist at me, and then asked me, in writing, why I painted that spot on the nose? I laughed outright; and soon mollified him by telling him that it was impossible for any live man to get upon the nose. I then explained my object, and the means of obtaining the correct distances for the proposed *fac-simile*. He then returned to the hotel, and reported to the proprietor, who afterward desired me to be quick, and remove the unsightly spot.

So, early the next morning, I again ascended the Mountain, this time in a dense cloud; and having removed the cloth, returned to the hotel in season for breakfast.

The visit to the head was repeated in a few days, and I then even ventured, more than once, *under the chin*, which proved extremely hazardous; and, but for my determination to get an accurate measurement, would have been quickly abandoned, as too risky for mortal man to undertake. I was told that no man had ever been known to go there before; but, whether true or not, I do not intend ever to risk my wife's husband's neck on any such desperate errand again; all the money in Wall Street would now be no allurement. I accomplished my task, and succeeded in getting, by various methods, the exact size and form of the various features which combine to form this most wonderful profile.

When I reported this last part of the adventure, no one was willing to believe that I had really been under the chin. Finding them so faithless, I offered to go once more, and prove my presence by building a fire under the chin, the smoke of which would be visible from the road. This I did; and then returning, without serious suffering, I was welcomed with amazement.

The spot I reached was directly under the chin, about twenty feet below it. If it had been possible to take along a short ladder, I could have gained foothold on a small projection, and touched the chin, which was about fifteen feet from the top to the neck, but it would have been extremely hazardous; for, if I had tripped ever so little, and lost my balance, I should have gone down the cliff some two thousand feet, and been dashed to pieces on the ragged rocks below. In case of such a termination, it is not likely that these sketches would ever have seen the light; and, after considering the matter of late, I am rather glad that I was preserved from falling.

I was very successful in making the desired model, and produced a truthful representation of the "Great Stone Face," for which I received the highest praise, and of which I made and sold a large number of copies.

The successful accomplishment of this undertaking rendered me quite famous in the Mountain region and there; are many who visited the Mountains that year, who greatly assisted me in disposing of copies of the model. Among these was one of the editors of the New York

Journal of Commerce, who gave me a "first-rate notice" in his gigantic newspaper, from which I extract the following:

"Mr. Wm. B. Swett, an ingenious deaf-mute, who has been employed for several summers at the Profile House, in the Franconia Mountains, and who is noted for his many adventures among them, produced, during the summer of 1866, a remarkable work,—a *fac-simile* of the Great Stone Face.

"It was made from actual measurement; taken at great risk of life and limb, he having been on the brow five times, and is said to be the first, and perhaps the only man, who ever ventured under the Chin, to get a correct view of the rocks which constitute the face.

"The fact is not generally known, that the 'Profile' is produced, not by the edge of one rock, but by the accidental grouping of a number of rocks, at various distances from each other.

"The front of the top of the precipice, which is about sixteen hundred feet high, is a group of rocks one hundred feet in breadth, and eighty feet high. The Nose is forty feet from the Forehead. The Mouth, which seems an opening of two thin lips, is a side-long chasm, or break, of fifty feet in extent.

"Viewed from the front, the Profile disappears, and can, indeed, only be seen from one point."

The Panther and Indian on Eagle Cliff.

Always on the look-out for opportunities to make a sensation, and add to the attraction of the localities, both for my own profit and that of the proprietors, I conceived the idea of placing a wooden panther high up on Eagle Cliff, facing the hotel.

After frequent visits to the Cliff, for the purpose of selecting a good place, and of calculating the distance, I went to work on my model. Aware that "distance lends enchantment to views," I drew the outlines roughly, and made it eighteen feet long, and large in proportion. It represented the animal in a crouching attitude, ready for a spring. I made it in nine pieces, using pine plank, one inch thick, for the purpose. Having matched and painted, or daubed these pieces to my satisfaction, I made nine secret visits to the selected spot, to which I had previously "blazed" a path, carrying one piece each time. I secreted the pieces in the bushes, and waited for the proper time. When the hotel was well filled with guests, myself and a boy went up one morning at three o'clock, and put the model together, nailing it firmly to trees, and bracing it well. The location was the brink of a precipice; and, during erection, I had to crawl around on its very edge, where there was so little foot-hold that I had a rope around my waist, the other end of which was lashed to a tree. After the model was up, it looked so rough and uncouth that I began to have misgivings as to the effect from the hotel; and having given it a few more daubs of paint, I hurried back, anxious to get the first view of it from the place. It was not yet six o'clock, and no one had yet appeared. Having assured myself that the model was rightly placed, looked quite natural, and could not fail to be noticed, I retired, to watch the effect, feeling highly gratified with my success. Some early risers soon appeared on the piazza, stretching themselves, rubbing their eyes, and expanding their lungs with copious inhalations of the keen, pure, and bracing Mountain air. Having cleared the night-mists from eye and brain, they proceeded to enjoy the prospect. One of them, looking in the direction of the Cliff, suddenly started, rubbed his eyes, and looked again, to be sure he was not deceived, and called the attention of the next to the model. Instantly, all was excitement; the more casual spectators apparently taking it for a reality, and the cry of "a panther! a panther!!" which rang through the house, soon brought all who were about to the piazza and front yard; while those yet in their rooms threw up their windows, and looked eagerly forth; telescopes and opera-glasses were brought into requisition, and soon settled the nature of the object, after which, the guests began to speculate as to the author of this exploit. The editor of the *New York Journal of Commerce*, who had some previous knowledge of me, decided that it must be my doing. He hunted me up, and asked me about it. I told him the whole story; whereupon he took me with him, and introduced me to the crowd, who listened with interest to his repetition of my story, voted the deed a success, and made up a handsome purse, which was presented to me as a token of their appreciation.

The next spring I returned, and found the panther still in its place. A visit to the spot proved it to be uninjured by the storms of the past winter, and I determined to put up the figure of an Indian with a gun, in the act of shooting the panther. I made the figure and the gun of the same material I had used in constructing the panther—inch-pine lumber.

The Indian was twenty feet high, and his gun was sixteen feet long, the barrel being eight inches wide. When I got the thing ready, I was very weak, from the effects of a bad cold, and was unable to conduct my operations as secretly as before. I, however, communicated my project to as few persons as possible, and got a gang of ten men to carry the pieces and the necessary implements, while I went with them to guide them to the spot, and to superintend operations. The day was hot, and the ascent rough, so that I was soon exhausted, and had to be helped on the way. Long before we arrived at our destination, I was almost dead for want of a drink of water. We had brought none with us, but discovered a place where water was oozing from the face of the rock. It did not come fast enough to give me a drink, and it was thinly spread over so

much surface that I could only moisten my parched lip and tongue.
Taking a bag, which I had with me, I half filled it with the soft moss of
the forest; and, by pressing the bag against the face of the rock, absorbed all the water that came. When the bag, by its increased weight,
appeared to contain a sufficient quantity, I applied my mouth to a corner,
compressed the bag with my hands, and obtained a copious and delicious
draught. Having satisfied my thirst, I again applied the bag to the
rock, filled it as full as possible, and resumed the ascent. The bag furnished several refreshing draughts of water before we reached the desired
place. It was necessary to locate the Indian at a considerable distance
from the panther, in order to secure the proper effect; and, as we could
not see the latter, it required several trips to and fro, and some nice
calculations; but we finally got it right, as observation from the hotel
afterwards proved. Having nailed it to the trees, and braced it firmly,
we returned to the Profile House, where the guests showed their appreciation of the enterprise by a second liberal collection. At latest accounts
during the summer of 1869, the panther and Indian still remained.

A Perilous Adventure.

One Saturday noon, after dinner, the other workmen and myself were
outside of the hotel, chatting and smoking, before resuming work, when
one of them asked me, in a bantering way, if I could ascend Eagle Cliff
directly from the hotel, instead of taking the usual roundabout way.
After some hesitation, I said I could do it, and would go if I could get
permission to leave work, and that I would fling out a white flag at the
top. All the lumber which we used had to be brought over the Mountains on teams, and it was slow and tedious work. This was before the
idea occurred to the proprietors to build a steam saw-mill, which was
afterwards done, and from which an ample supply was furnished. As
we happened to be out of lumber at the time, I readily obtained leave
of absence.

Procuring a table-cloth and some stout twine, and taking neither coat,
axe, or lunch, as usual — so confident was I that I should need none of
them — I plunged into the woods, about two o'clock, P. M., and commenced the ascent. The day was warm; the work uncomfortable; and
the midgets, or wood-flies, more troublesome than ever. I had to keep
my hands constantly in motion about my face to keep them off; their bite
being always annoying, and often poisonous. The ascent became more
and more difficult, and I made up my mind that it was a mad work to get
to the top; but, to think of returning, was not pleasant, as the boys would
laugh at me. I might take the usual way, and no one be the wiser; but
that would be a cheat, and so I kept on. I had often to scramble up on my
hands and knees, and to pull myself up by roots and bushes, and be

very cautious about it, as they had no firm hold in the ground, and were easily pulled up. A bush suddenly gave way in one place, and, had not a large tree prevented it. I should have had a serious fall upon the jagged rocks twenty feet below. It was now impossible to descend, for I was on a ledge from which no downward path was visible. Working my way up, with immense labor, I at last discovered a huge crack or fissure, some thirty feet long, two feet wide, and ten feet high, with several trees growing in it, and I squeezed myself up and through it. At its end I was glad to see that I was near the top, which I quickly gained. While resting from the fatigue induced by my exertions, I was troubled with unpleasant doubts about a safe return; but I dismissed them for the present, and, climbing the tallest tree I could find, I obtained a truly sublime view. The tree waved gently to and fro in the wind with a soothing effect; Lafayette lifted seat far toward the sky, and far below me was the Profile House, looking no larger than a bird-house, such as are often set up by boys. I longed to have some of my friends present to share my delight. I tied the table-cloth out on the branches, and immediately the guests and workmen began to congregate in front of the hotel, and to wave their handkerchiefs, to show that they saw that I had really reached the top, although they probably had not expected to see me make my appearance in the top of a tree. Descending from the tree, after an hour of true enjoyment, I was soon convinced that it was impossible to return by the way I had come, and that my only course was to make the best of my way to the columnar crag, and search for a path down its side. The distance was only half a mile, but the undergrowth was so thick, and fallen trees so numerous, that my progress was very slow. I now repented not having brought my hand-axe, with which to cut my way through. The pitiless midgets followed me in clouds; I never smoke, or I could easily have kept them off. I have tried mosquito-netting around my head and face, but found it to answer no good purpose, as, besides being easily torn, it interfered with the frequent necessity of wiping away the perspiration, and was otherwise uncomfortable.

From the brink of the crag, to which I finally attained, I had another glorious view of the hills; a small part of the chin of the "Old Man" could be seen, but nothing of the nose, mouth, or forehead. I built a small fire in a hole in the rock, both to drive off the midgets and attract the attention of those below. The crowd soon saw the smoke, and the waving of handkerchiefs was repeated.

I had stepped on a piece of rock to have a better view, and, as I turned to get down, I felt it move; with a sudden spring, I grasped a bush, and fell flat upon my breast, while the stone rolled over, and went thundering down the precipice. I wished to get down the cliff, it is true, but not in that hasty fashion, as I came near doing. Putting out the fire, a precaution the importance of which I would impress upon all who build fires in the woods, the neglect of it having caused many extensive conflagrations, I resumed my search for a way down. During this time, a pair of large owls flew up from the depths below, fluttered blindly about for a moment or two, and then dove down again. I am not superstitious, otherwise the appearance of these birds, considered of evil omen, at such a time and place, might have depressed my already heavy spirits. After a long search, I found I was in a tight place, and saw no other way out of it than to go down the opposite side of the cliff, and ascend Mount Lafayette.

Viewed from a distance, the deep, black ravine that scars the Mountain-side seemed easy of ascent ; a complete deception, as will be seen. Once at the top of the ravine, I could easily gain the well-known bridle-path, and from that point the way was clear. I should also have another extensive view, and it was rare for one to get three different views, from points so far apart, on the same day. I was admonished to make haste, as the sun, considering the distance I had yet to go and the probable and possible difficulties of the way, was unpleasantly near setting.

I ran, jumped and slid as far as the bottom of the valley, where I stopped to quench my thirst in a clear, sparkling brook which ran there, built a fire to keep the midgets away, and sat down to rest a little, contemplating, meanwhile, the yawning blackness of the ravine, which was now directly in front of me, and looked gloomy enough, but its very gloom was sublime.

As soon as I got well rested, I commenced the ascent in earnest. I was frequently obliged to cross and re-cross the rushing brook ; the sides were very steep, and trees and bushes were scattered here and there, but the ravine was mostly lined, as far as one could see, with large and small stones, from which the rains had washed away the earth, until many of them stood ready to roll down at a touch, or even at a heavy jar. The sun shone straight into the chasm, and the lofty sides kept the wind away : the heat was almost suffocating, and before long most of my clothing was saturated with perspiration. The ascent, comparatively easy at first, became more difficult every moment, and the heat more oppressive : to think of stopping was out of the question, as eight miles still lay between myself and the Profile House. Detention, by darkness, would very likely be death. I could not shorten the distance by climbing the side, for the underbrush was impenetrable without an axe. So I pushed along, painfully : I was much fatigued and excited ; my feet were sore ; the soles of my shoes, new the day before, being worn through. I began to fear I could not extricate myself from the ravine, and I prayed for deliverance as I had never prayed before ; thoughts of my family, and of my past life, flashed through my mind.

It is remarkable how rapidly and clearly a man can think when in danger ; in what a short space of time every act of his life, good or bad, passes in review before him.

About this time, I stepped on a loose rock, which slid from under my feet, and rolled heavily downward, starting numerous other rocks in its course, and raising an immense cloud of dust. I soon discovered a new source of danger ; the jar, and the reverberations of the rolling stones below me, had started those above, and they now rolled past in considerable numbers, some of them passing quite near me. The rock on which I now stood — to which I had sprung when the other gave way — was quite slippery, and I could not move out of the way should any of the stones come in my direction, lest I lose my footing and follow them to the bottom.

The ravine above and ahead of me was steep, and quite smooth. Looking up, to see how long the commotion was likely to last, I saw a huge rock far up the slope, coming directly down upon me at a fearful speed. I also noticed that a large rock cropped out ten or twelve feet above my head, and that the coming stone would hit it, and, in all probability, fetch both upon me, and hurl me to destruction. Mentally bidding farewell to the world, and commending my spirit to God, I kept my eyes fixed on the rock. It struck the projection — which proved to be a solid spur in the Mountain-side, and consequently did not move — bounded over my head, and went spinning to the bottom, where it flew into a thousand pieces.

A few more stones passed me, and then all became quiet again. I cannot describe my feelings at this deliverance : but I imagine I know how a man feels who has been reprieved at the foot of the gallows.

I now took courage, and resumed the ascent, picking my way up carefully. Farther on, I came to a broad, flat rock, steep, wet and slippery. Being unable to go around it on either side, I went down on hands and knees and crawled up its surface. Reaching what I thought a safe place, I attempted to stand upright. My feet slipped, and I fell on my face, bruising myself considerably. I slid on and down till my eye caught a little crack in the rock, into which I got the ends of my fingers, and thus stopped the descent, though it seemed only a postponement of the inevitable end ; for of course I could not hold on forever. I could not move ; the clouds of midgets which had followed me all along, now seemed to know that their opportunity had come, and settled in a mass on my neck, face and hands. The torment was terrible, but I was helpless.

Over the surface of the rock on which I was spread out, the water trickled from a spring above, and I was soon quite wet. If I was obliged to stay out all night, my only safety was in having a good fire. Since leaving the last place where I had made a fire, I had discovered that I laid my matches on the ground, while lighting it, and left them there; and that I had but one solitary match, which was in my vest pocket. My greatest fear now was, that this one match would get wet, and I be thus reduced to extremity.

Looking carefully around, I saw a crevice, not far from my feet, into which, if I could get my feet, I could resume my progress on hands and knees. The length of my legs, inconvenient at times, now did me good service, as they could just reach it. Cautiously letting go my hold with one hand, and finding it was safe, I indulged in a savage sweep at the midgets on my face, giving me a slight relief. A little exertion enabled me to get out of my dangerous situation, crawl away, continue my upward progress, and reach the strange-looking rock near the top of the Mountain, known as the " Altar," where I dropped on the moss, utterly exhausted, but very thankful that the worst was over.

A little dirty water helped to revive me. The sun was near setting — it had set long ago to those in the valleys below — and the air, clearer than at any of my previous visits, afforded me a most magnificent view, the beauty of which chained me to my seat, till the light began to fade away. My one match proved to have fortunately remained unwet, and the descent of the Mountain, by the bridle-path, now began.

The sharp stones hurt my feet, and my progress was not rapid; when the woods below the cone of the Mountain were reached, the darkness rendered further progress dangerous without a light; the idea of a night in the woods was rejected; a pile of white birch-bark was collected, and a torch made; the one match, upon the ignition of which so much depended, was drawn, with a prayer for success; the torch blazed forth, and by its light the foot of the Mountain was reached at last. Then followed a long rest on the grass at the side of the road, rendered doubly sweet by a knowledge that the danger was passed, and only two miles of smooth travel now intervened.

The hotel was finally reached, and it is doubted if a more famished tatterdemalion was ever seen within its walls than entered them about ten o'clock that night, and sank helplessly on a chair.

My entrance cut short the speculations, and allayed the anxieties, of all concerned. Every attention was rendered; a bountiful supper was furnished, and, after doing it ample justice, I was glad to crawl off to bed. The next day, a full account of the adventure, on my part, and a liberal collection on that of the guests, ended the matter for the present. I was so lame that I had to sit down all day, and was unable to work.

THIRD SUMMER.

Ice Blockade on the Ammonoosuc.

EARLY in the spring, I was again called to return to the Profile House. Bitter experience, in former seasons, had taught me that I might expect snow-storms and wintry weather, and so I took the precaution to be provided for such contingencies. A thick riding-blanket and warm mittens are excellent companions on such a journey.

Arriving at Franconia by stage, from Littleton, I was not a little amazed to find solid cakes of ice, large and small, scattered all over the town, in the fields, gardens, and orchards, not omitting the open doors of barns and sheds. Some of the front doors of the dwellings were completely blocked up, and the whole appearance of things generally was most singular. It appeared as if the spirits of the Mountains had been having a grand *mêlée*, the weapons being cakes of ice. I am not sure which side beat. Upon inquiring into the cause of this strange appearance, I learned that a sudden freshet had taken place on the Ammonoosuc River, caused by the snow melting along the ravine of Mount Lafayette, and the water had rushed down, breaking the ice in the river into fragments, which were carried all over the town when an ice-jam occurred, which kept the water back, and submerged the town some three feet. This accounted for the ice in such unusual places. The road had been cleared out to make travelling possible.

While we were preparing to go forward, we were suddenly overtaken by a violent snow-storm, which came almost unheralded. We were prepared for it — our stout blankets keeping us comfortable — but the snow very soon became too deep for the stage to proceed on wheels, so we were obliged to halt, and hold a consultation.

We determined to go on, in spite of the storm, provided we could find some sort of a sled large enough to take us all along. There were about a dozen of us, all told, and not afraid of the weather. After considerable search, we procured a wood-sled belonging to a farmer near by; and having hitched our horses to it, and enveloped ourselves in our blankets and buffalo-robes, the driver cracked his whip, and off we started in high glee. The way was rather uncertain, but soon the storm ceased, almost as suddenly as it commenced, and we had a splendid moonlight ride through the gloomy forest, arriving safely at the Profile House. Here a rousing fire and a hot supper soon put us to rights, and the evening passed in great good humor. The next morning's sun revealed . snow-drifts reaching twenty feet in height.

A Visit to the Other Side of " Cannon Mountain."

I started off, one day, with the intention of visiting the scene of the great conflagration caused by a fire kindled by some careless company of gentlemen, in the woods, years ago, on the other side of " Cannon Mountain." Ascending by the path which leads to its top, I soon reached it, and struck into the pathless woods, coming out, after a while, directly upon the place I sought. It was a desolate waste, of fifteen square miles ; a wilderness of jagged and shattered rocks, charred stumps, and tangled briars, upon which the sun beat down in unobstructed fervor, making the place a very purgatory. The purgatorial appearance of the place was much increased by the presence of clouds of midgets, (wood-flies,) which pursued me with unrelenting vigor throughout my visit, obliging me to keep one hand continually in motion, to defend myself from their attacks. I had intended to explore the place sufficiently to obtain a fair idea of it, and then retrace my steps. I picked my way up and down, over and among the rocks, many of which were of immense size, and all looked as if rent and scattered by some great convulsion of nature, for angular shapes were universal ; there not being a round, naturally-shaped rock within the range of my vision. Coming to a place where the rocks shot sheer down for several feet, I jumped off without due calculation, and the impetus of the leap carried me much farther than I had intended to go. When I finally brought up, I found myself in a sort of amphitheatre, the open side of it being directly ahead of me in the direction I had been pursuing, while above and behind me, the steep ascent forbade return. I had, therefore, to keep on, and trust to reaching the woods at the foot of the Mountain, through which I must find my way, in a roundabout direction, to the hotel.

The rocks around me abounded in remarkable resemblances to such things as tombs, pulpits, water-wheels, etc., and but a slight stretch of the imagination was necessary to conjure up many other things, even animals and persons, from the maze of fantastical shapes around. It was impossible to make haste, so I proceeded at a slow pace, stopping now and then to examine whatever attracted my attention ; sending rocks down the steep places, to see them fly to splinters at the bottom, and otherwise amusing myself. I finally reached the woods, after a tiresome tramp, and, in their cool shade, I stopped to rest and eat my luncheon. Having duly refreshed myself, I took observations, and plunged into the woods in the direction of home. After getting several falls, tearing my clothes to tatters, and being several times at fault, I found myself in a familiar locality, and had no further trouble in getting home.

An Avalanche on " Bald Mountain."

In reviewing my visit to the desolate region referred to above, my rolling of rocks down the steeps, and the effects thereof, made me desirous of witnessing the same thing on a grander scale.

I remembered, in one of my visits to "Bald Mountain," so called from its lofty top being round and bare, to have seen an immense boulder of granite standing upright, quite near the brink of a long, steep incline which shot clear from the top of the Mountain to the line of fore t, and far below it. I thought it would be fun to roll that boulder down the steep; but, how to do it? I paid two or three visits to the spot, to calculate the possibility of starting it, and to ascertain what implements were necessary, and how many hands would be required. Having completed my arrangements, I broached the subject to some of the workmen. It was a Saturday afternoon, and work was dull. The idea was readily taken up, and a party of seven men, besides myself, started for the top of the Mountain, distant about five miles. We carried wooden levers. Arriving at the spot, we arranged our implements, and applied them at the proper place, having first tried our united strength on it, and found it immovable. As the lever was steadily applied to the rock, it gradually yielded; and, as soon as its balance was sufficiently disturbed to insure its going over, a sharp, quick jerk was given to the bar, and we scattered instantly, turning, as soon as we reached a safe distance, to watch the effect. The rock turned over slowly once or twice, and then, gathering headway at each revolution, it thundered down the slope at a fearful rate of speed, raising great clouds of smoke and dust, and drawing streams of fire from the rocks, over which it tore its way. We saw it reach the forest line, and we saw the tall trees go down before it like grass before the mower's scythe. It disappeared from view, leaving a long, broad avenue behind it. That rock was the most speedy and effective path-maker that I ever saw. After all was over, I followed the trail of the rock down the slope, and was astonished at the ruin it had wrought. It was exactly as if a tornado had been along.

Retracing my steps, I joined the rest in a lunch; having finished it, we went leisurely back to the Profile House, well satisfied with the result of our afternoon's frolic.

Walker's Falls.

These Falls, although well worth seeing, and comparatively easy of access with a competent guide, are yet neglected by the great majority of tourists. In fact, judged by the general practice of visitors, to have been *to* the Mountains is one thing, to have been *over* them — to have "done" them — is quite another.

I have already related how I went in search of the gentleman who got lost in the attempt to find these Falls without a guide, and the incidents connected therewith. The next spring I went with a gumming party to guide them to the Falls. The Mountains are covered mostly with spruce-trees, on which chewing-gum can be found in abundance, especially on the sunny side of the hills. Parties often go after gum. They carry poles about eight feet long, having chisels fastened to the smaller end, with which to cut off the gum when found high up the trees. The return of such a party, and the distribution of the gum, causes an amount of chewing that would astonish a cow. The distance from the Profile House was about five miles. There was enough snow still on the ground to render it difficult to find the true path, and leaves and dead branches had been strewed around so thickly the previous winter, as to increase the perplexity of a first passage, to the extent of making the way rather devious. I was several times at fault; and, most of the party getting tired out, voted to return, which they did, and got lost, caught in a heavy shower, and were thoroughly soaked long before they struck the road leading to the hotel. Two of the party pushed on, taking me with them: we soon found the path, and shortly arrived at the Falls, in viewing which we found ample satisfaction for coming. Sated with views of the rushing waters, and the surrounding scenery from various points, we finally turned into the woods in search of gum. One of us struck the fresh track of a deer, and, entirely forgetting the coming storm, which had been gradually darkening the air for some time, we gave chase, hoping to see the animal. We continued the pursuit until the heavy pattering of the rain brought us to our senses. Halting on the top of a slight elevation, we saw that we were completely lost. My two companions now wished that they had returned with the main body of the party, although, as it afterwards appeared, had they done so without me they would have been no better off. After some search, I saw a landmark which had a familiar look, and was sure that, by taking a downward direction, we should strike the bridle-path. The other two, however, insisted on going in the opposite direction, and I deferred to them so far as to let them try it, although I was morally certain that we should become still more involved in the mazes of the forest. They went up and down for two hours, without success, and then gave it up. By this time we were thoroughly wet and tired. Turning about, and bidding them follow, I sped down the side of the Mountain as straight as possible, through mud, mire, and bushes, over rocks, stumps, and logs, dodging here and there to avoid the trees, and gaining impetus at every step, until we reached the low lands, where I looked about for a running stream, knowing that if I could find one I could easily tell, by the direction in which it ran, which way to go. Finding one, we followed it down, and soon came to a familiar path, which led us safely out of the difficulty. Had the two men been left to themselves, it would probably have been a "gone case" with them.

A few weeks after this I went out again, with the intention of examining the Falls, and more thoroughly exploring their neighborhood. I was advised not to go, as the weather threatened to be bad; but, even while admitting the fact, I went. I reached the foot of the Falls, and had commenced the ascent, when I discovered a violent thunder-storm approaching. There was a cave situated in the side of the cliff, which was called Lion's Cave, some eighty rods above my head, which promised shelter if I could reach it in season. I hastened up the steep ascent, much of the way on my hands and knees, until I had nearly reached it, when my progress was barred by a chasm, not visible from below. One side of the chasm was higher than the other; and, taking my hatchet from my belt, I felled and roughly trimmed a stout sapling, which I laid across the chasm, and which, half-ladder, half-bridge, enabled me to cross and gain the coveted shelter. I had imagined it to be a huge cleft in the rock, but it proved to be only about six feet deep, and not high enough for me to stand up in, although I could sit comfortably, and be perfectly sheltered. The shower burst soon; the rain drove in sheets across the valley below me; it poured down from the Mountain above, forming a thick, unbroken curtain before the mouth of the cave; a miniature Niagara, in fact, which tossed and tumbled down the slope into the brook below, now swollen to a river. I enjoyed the scene vastly; but the omnipresent midgets soon found me out, and attacked me, seriously interfering with my pleasure, and forcing me to make a fire and smoke them out. In the course of an hour, the shower ceased as suddenly as it had begun. Descending from my elevated perch, and deferring my intended explorations to a future time, I went home, and was jeered and laughed at for my folly, until they discovered that my clothes were dry, when they stopped laughing, and desired particulars, which I gave them.

At another time, an old lady insisted on visiting the Falls, and engaged me as guide. In company with several men and two ladies, she hired a team, and set out. When the party reached the spot where persons wishing to visit the Falls must alight, and take the foot-path, all except the old lady had changed their minds, and decided to keep on and visit the Basin. She adhered to her original intention, and, after ordering the team to wait for her on its return, she jumped out, and I followed her, the rest of the party going on. Looking up, previous to entering the woods, I saw that one of the sudden storms peculiar to Mountain regions had stolen upon us unawares, was rearing its crest above the tree-tops, and would soon burst upon us. If those who had gone on should see the storm in season, they would return at full speed; but that would not save any of us from a drenching, and I determined to risk being left for the present, and shelter my companion. Calling her attention to the storm, she readily comprehended that we could not visit the Falls, and signified her willingness to go wherever I chose. I led her away some distance into the woods, to a broad, overhanging rock, which I had noticed in a previous ramble, underneath which I fixed seats for her and myself, and got snugly settled just as the shower came on. The thunder roared; the lightning flashed; the tall forest-trees bowed and writhed under the violence of the wind, and the rain fell in torrents; but we were safe and dry, and could calmly look out and enjoy the really sublime spectacle. The old lady was in high glee at the thought of the miserable plight in which the rest of the party must necessarily be, without protection of any kind. After the rain had passed away, she listened for the team, and when she heard it coming up the road, we proceeded to its side and waited for it to come up. It was a sorry-looking company that we beheld,— all wet, draggled, and woe-begone; and we laughed heartily, both at their appearance and at their unfeigned astonishment at our dry and comfortable condition. We got in, and dashed away for the hotel, where our wet companions hurried off in search of dry clothing and fires. The old lady stood up all the way, declining to sit down where everything was soaked, and she chuckled right merrily, to think that insisting on going to the Falls had saved her from a wetting.

Fireworks on *Profile Lake.*

It had become a regular custom for those guests who had passed the season at the Profile House, to get up some sort of a party or pic-nic before separating, as a fitting close for their holiday season. I almost always had a hand in the arrangements, for the hotel-keeper generally recommended me as a handy-man on such occasions. Being somewhat ready-witted, and withal not afraid of a little hard work, I usually managed to give satisfaction.

Once I had been requested to make preparations for a jolly good time at the old Flume House, which was then unoccupied. A party of about fifty ladies and gentlemen proposed to have a supper and ball, and I was somewhat nonplussed to arrange for their comfort, as there was no furniture in the building, and it was six miles distant from the Profile House. However, at it I went, cutting up fence-boards for tables, and made seats by the aid of work-benches. The dining-hall I decorated with evergreen as well as I could, and made it look quite respectable. Many delicacies had been sent all the way from New York, and the other viands were procured from the Profile House.

By dint of hard work, I managed to get all ready for company; and in the afternoon a long line of carriages appeared, with flags flying and music playing. The party was received with due ceremony, and ushered into the parlors, where they deposited their extra clothing. Then came a hop, and afterwards a large fire was built outside, where some green corn was roasted in a primitive manner. When all things were ready, the party was ushered into the dining-hall, and were much surprised at the appearance of the tables. Every one seemed to enjoy the scene, and made the hall ring with their jokes and laughter. Then came toasts and speeches, the leader of the party occupying an old wagon-seat which I found in the barn. Their merry-making lasted until midnight, when all returned to the Profile House, highly gratified with their entertainment, and unanimously voting that the whole occasion was a decided success, even if it was improvised by a deaf-mute.

But there was another occasion which, while the management of it bothered my brains somewhat, yet proved to be a very agreeable and brilliant affair.

At a distance of about eighty rods from the hotel is a pretty sheet of water, called Profile Lake; or, more properly, "The Old Man's Washbowl." Surrounded by high hills and a dense forest, it has a most sombre appearance, particularly at night. The idea was started by a gentleman from New York, connected with the *Journal of Commerce*, and another from Philadelphia, of having a row on the lake at night, with a grand display of fireworks. When asked if I understood how to manage the rockets, etc., I had to plead partial ignorance; but did not doubt that I could make a proper display with a little instruction. So the whole arrangement of the night's display was left to me, and a busy time I had of it for two days; the fireworks had been ordered from Boston, and arrived in due time. Procuring all the boats that could be found on Echo Lake and Profile Lake, eighteen in all, we had them cleaned, and fitted up with a Chinese lantern at each end. I went to the other end of the lake, about a quarter of a mile from the boat-house, and prepared a big pile of dry and green boughs, twigs and brush, all ready for a bonfire. Then I had a large ball, some two feet in diameter, made of rags, well smeared with tar, fastened to the top of a pole about twelve feet high, which I set on a boat made from an old barn-door, and anchored it in the middle of the lake.

When the evening came, I was all ready for our grand celebration. Before the select party who were to occupy the boats arrived, with the assistance of one man, I had all the Chinese lanterns lighted up with sperm candles, presenting a very pretty spectacle. Then came the party down the road, headed by a band of music, and followed by nearly all the guests from the hotel who wished to witness the novel scene. Our brilliant fleet of boats was quickly filled by the ladies and gentlemen, with the band, while I had gone out into the lake in a boat, with one assistant to help me about the rockets, which I fired from time to time amid the cheers of the spectators. The effect was very brilliant, for the night was very dark, and no stars appeared to interfere with the general

effect. The glare of the rockets and Roman candles presented a magnificent, yet peculiarly sombre appearance, which quite astonished the
spectators, who fairly yelled with delight. I could see by the light of
the lanterns, that the party in the boats were quite excited, waving their
handkerchiefs and huzzaing.

I now pushed off to the pile of brush and lighted it, and quickly
rowed away, so that I might not be seen. It soon worked up into a
strong blaze, causing the flames to ascend some forty feet; this had a
novel effect, lighting up the whole lake. After this had subsided, I set
fire to the grand illuminator on the float, which I did by means of a rag
saturated with oil, at the end of a long stick; at the same time setting
the raft to rocking, so that the pole appeared to wave to and fro, like
a vessel on a high sea. The effect of this was very brilliant, also, and it
burned quite a while. The performance closed with another display
of fireworks, the various colors having a peculiarly beautiful effect with
such weird surroundings. The party appeared to be satisfied with the
entertainment, and rowing back to the boat-house, they landed, taking
the Chinese lanterns for company, marched back to the hotel, enlivening
the way with songs and cheers. On arriving at the hotel a sumptuous
supper was in readiness, and a hop in the grand saloon closed the
evening's amusement. I received many thanks for my part of the performance, and I look back with much pleasure upon that evening spent
on Profile Lake.

One incident somewhat marred the enjoyment of one of the party, —
a lady, who disdained any assistance on leaving the boat. Being
rather stout and solid, she contrived, while standing upon the edge of
the boat and trying to spring upon the platform, to push the boat away
from it, and her ladyship fell plump into the water. She was quickly
rescued, but thoroughly soaked; and quite disgusted with the sudden
change of scene. Hurrying to the hotel, she was quickly arrayed in dry
clothing, and means to be a little more careful next time.

The next morning one of the guests, seeing the preparations for leaving by so many of his friends, concluded to attempt one more piece of
fun; and so, before the stages were ready, he called me to his aid with
half a dozen others of the employés. He rigged us up in grotesque
costumes, consisting of the oldest and oddest garments that could be
found. Guns, brooms, or wooden swords furnished our armament; and
with huge pieces of tin upon our breasts, we presented an appearance much
like Falstaff's brave army. Thus equipped as genuine country police, we
waited in a side-room until the stages began to fill up, when we suddenly
marched out, and going directly into the office of the hotel, pretended
that there had been some pickpockets at work. We arrested several
of the most prominent of the party, and took them into one of the public
rooms, where we searched them, and made a pretence of finding the lost

wallets. A mock trial was commenced at once; and it being soon discovered that it was all a sham, the evidence proceeded, to the great amusement of the bystanders. The jury finally acquitted the prisoners of any positive act of wrong-doing, and they were dismissed by the learned judge, with an injunction to be careful and never do so again, or the majesty of the law might visit them with some punishment awful to contemplate. This farce over, the departing guests gave us a round of cheers, and they rolled away to the duties and cares of life in the outside world.

After so much fun and amusement, I found it rather hard to settle down again to daily labor; but the summer was passing, and there was work to be done before cold weather should put an embargo on our labors. So I soon settled down to it, and gave my brains a resting-spell, while my hands and tools found plenty to do to keep off any sense of loneliness.

⊰ ⬩ ⊱

MY LAST ADVENTURE, AND A TRIP AROUND THE MOUNTAINS.

As cold weather was approaching, and the work so far completed to the satisfaction of the proprietor of the hotel, all the workmen were dismissed, and informed their services would not be required next year; so I concluded on bidding adieu to the Mountains.

I had calculated on making further explorations, in other inaccessible places, if I had time and opportunity, but finally gave up the idea, getting somewhat wearied of the "Adventures." I therefore turned my thoughts to Boston, as the most suitable field for me to labor in for the welfare of the Deaf-Mutes; but before taking my final leave, I decided on a trip around the White Mountains, intending to make the best use of my time.

Packing up my tools and trunk, I forwarded them home, not wishing to encumber myself with anything but a warm blanket. The prospect of a pleasant journey — one hundred and thirty miles — was very cheering, as the weather was unusually pleasant for the season of the year. Bidding adieu to all my friends at the hotel, I jumped on top of the stage-coach, not caring to ride inside; if I had done so, many beautiful views would have been lost sight of. My first stopping-place was at Bethlehem; I made my way to the Bethlehem Hotel, where I met an old friend, who had been famous among the mountain people for his daring adventures, far eclipsing my own. It was he who offered to bet a sum of money that he would wheel a bag of corn, on a wheelbarrow, to Plymouth, thirty miles up and down hills, on condition, if he should win, that the loser should pay the stake, and provide him with a situation in one of the hotels. He was successful in his undertaking, though it was a very arduous task, taking a day and a half to accomplish. He rested at the Profile House the night he performed his feat. The wheelbarrow he used was decorated and varnished, and hung up in a conspicuous place in the hotel, with his name inscribed on it, as a reward for his triumph.

The view, as seen from the Bethlehem Hotel, was very fine, and in the distance loomed up Mount Washington, the direction which I intended to take. Leaving Bethlehem, we were pleasantly jogging along when suddenly, almost, a heavy rain-storm set in. Two of the men who sat on top with me jumped off, and got inside the coach, which was already full, leaving me to keep company with the driver. I was not in the least discomfited, but wrapped myself up snugly in my blanket, and pulled down the rim of my hat, and in a few moments I was drenched through and through. Not having any change of clothing with me, I was in a sorry plight, but resolved to make the best of it. In a short time the storm abated, and the sun shone out beautifully, and by its heat I partially dried my clothes, and soon reached the White Mountain House, where half an hour was allowed for changing horses, which I availed myself of by getting thoroughly dry in the kitchen.

After a ride of thirty miles I reached the Crawford House, and was immediately recognized by several who knew me, and invited to stay there, free of all charge. Not having time to spare, I hastened back three miles to the depot of the railroad up Mount Washington, and had the satisfaction of examining the engine and track; but was sorely disappointed at not having a chance to ride up, though fully satisfied of the greatness of its undertaking. Early next morning, before the guests were up, I had some lunch ready; and, with my cane for a companion, determined to take a day's tramp, and visit the Elephant. The outline of the rock shows the head, ear, proboscis and mouth. The Silver Cascade is a beautiful fall; the Pulpit is a curious, towering rock, by the foot of the mountain; the Old Maid of the Mount, and the Young Man of the Mountain, the Infant and the Wiley House, so famous in history for the destruction of a whole family of seven by an avalanche of snow and rock, were examined minutely, affording me much pleasure.

The Old Maid and the Young Man disappointed me somewhat, for I had an idea their faces were as attractive as "The Old Man." The outlines were not half as good as my old *friend's*. The Devil's Den, the Apron, and other places of interest were visited. I was not in the least molested by the midgets, as they had nearly disappeared with the approach of cold weather. The Wiley House is a very interesting place to visit; it contains several articles which belonged to the ill-fated family before mentioned, such as a table, crockery-ware, boots, hats, guns, etc. In most of the rooms the names of visitors are written all over the walls. I inscribed my name high up on the wall, having the advantage, in height, over most of the guests. I visited the spot where the unfortunate family are buried, and the great rock that rolled down the mountain. It seems they had been deceived by the echoes of the rolling avalanche, and fled in the wrong direction ; they would have been saved had they gone across the road, on the opposite side. Their house stood uninjured.

Having satisfied my curiosity, I made my way back to the Crawford House, a distance of six miles. The sun was setting, and a rain-storm approaching from behind the mountain. Being three miles from the hotel, or any house to shelter me, I did not like the idea of being drenched, as I was before, by the Rain Fiend, as I called it ; and fortunately I discovered a projecting rock a few rods from where I stood, and fled to it, barely reaching it before the rain poured down in torrents. I chuckled over my luck, for I always considered myself a lucky fellow. The rain over, I was glad to come out with dry clothes. I soon reached the hotel, and ate a hearty supper, for I was " as hungry as a wolf."

The next morning I met a man of whom I had some knowledge, who had been guide and servant at the Profile House. He was poor when I first knew him, but now he wore gold and diamond rings, and was very fashionably dressed. He had just married a rich heiress, from New York. It seems he was acting as a guide up Mount Washington, and amongst the party was a lady on horseback, who, at first sight, became violently enamored of him. After some billing and cooing, they were married, and he now rides in a two-horse carriage. He was a lucky fellow, indeed, and I wished myself in his place ; but, on second thought, I remembered I had a loving wife, which is far better than a rich heiress.

The ride up Mount Washington had been entirely stopped, on account of the great danger of being caught in frost-clouds, which sadly disappointed me, for I desired to see the Tip Top House, and all the surrounding hills, but especially the monument of Lizzie Bourne, in whose fate I felt a lively interest. She had gone up with her uncle, a doctor, late in the season, and late in the afternoon, without a guide, and contrary to the advice of their friends. They both got lost in their ascent, and wandered about till dark. She had gone out of the path, and wandered among the bushes and shrubs, until nearly all her clothes were torn off; and, unable to stand the cold, she fell down and died. The doctor was discovered, nearly frozen, keeping guard over her, and was rescued. She was greatly mourned, and her remains were sent home. A monument was erected to her memory by her friends, with rocks found on the spot where she died.

It had been my intention to cross the Mountain to the Glen House, but I was dissuaded from it, no guide being willing to risk going up with me. To think of further stay would prove of no advantage to me, so I decided to hurry home direct, instead of carrying out my plan, and was sadly disappointed. I bade good-by to the Crawford House, and took stage direct to Centre Harbor. One little incident I witnessed, which I shall never forget: As we were riding down a hill, I noticed a beautiful girl sitting on a chair, a rod or more from a lonely dwelling-house by the road-side, holding a pan in her lap, and in it were some blackberries in boxes of white birch. She was waiting the approach of stages to sell berries to passengers, as had been her custom. The horses were a little unmanageable, and the driver tried to stop them, putting his foot on the break to allow the passengers to dismount and purchase the berries; but the whiffle-tree behind the horses knocked her over, and spilled them all. I discovered she had but one leg. She was an exceedingly pretty girl, and her head was covered with a profusion of curls. Fortunately she was not hurt; but being unable to stand up, and overpowered with grief at the loss of her berries, it was truly pitiable to see her. All the passengers heartily sympathized with her: they jumped out, raised her up, and kissed her, lifting her on her chair. Her hands were soon well-filled with money, to compensate her for the fright and loss. She was as meek as she was beautiful. How she came to lose her leg, I never learnt.

Reaching the Centre House, and crossing Winnipiseogee Lake on the steamer *Lady of the Lake*, I took the cars and reached home, highly gratified with my Three Summers' Adventures.

BOSTON
DEAF-MUTE LIBRARY ASSOCIATION.

This enterprise, inaugurated by the Deaf-Mutes, has proved of much benefit to them as a distinct class of our citizens. Their numbers in and about the city are considerable ; and, deprived as they are by nature of many of the ordinary modes of enjoyment of their fellows, it meets a want before unprovided for. They do not wish to be always at home, and more especially in their boarding-places, where they seldom find any one willing to take time to correspond with them. They need the same relaxation and social enjoyment as others more favored by nature.

Most of the Deaf-Mutes in Boston are from the country, and are all the more impressible by the sights of the city. The Public Library is not the place for them, because they are not at home there. They need some place where positive contact with their brother and sister mutes will tend to develop their minds, which must be exercised to be of use.

The object of the Library Association is to provide a pleasant Reading-Room and Lecture-Hall for all Deaf-Mutes, where they can meet their companions, read the papers and books, attend lectures, enjoy pictures, and talk as much as they please ; — for it is a blessed boon so to do.

Their rooms, at No. 289 Washington Street, are convenient, attractive, and comfortable, and will be improved as opportunity offers.

Various plans are in contemplation for extending its usefulness to all the Deaf-Mutes, resident or travelling.

OFFICERS.

THE proceeds arising from the sale of this Pamphlet, go to the fund of the Boston Deaf-Mute Mission.

Please take one or more.

Price 25 Cents.

Any Donations for the Mission will be gratefully received.

Periodical Dealers can be supplied with this Pamphlet at wholesale price.

Send all orders, with address, to Wm. B. Swett, Library Room, 289 Washington Street, Boston, Mass., to which prompt attention will be given.

DEAF-MUTE ALPHABET.

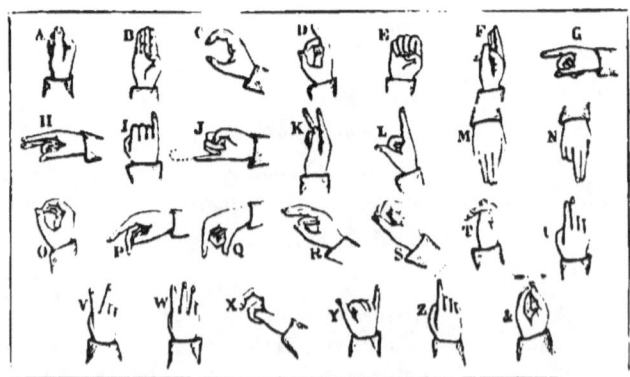

www.ingramcontent.com/pod-product-compliance
Lightning Source LLC
Chambersburg PA
CBHW030902260626
47169CB00008B/2642